Thunderbolt

Little Lightning

Cruella

Lars

Jasper Baddun

Horace Baddun

Published by Scholastic Inc.,
90 Old Sherman Turnpike, Danbury, Connecticut 06816.

For information regarding permission, write to:
Disney Licensed Publishing,
114 Fifth Avenue, New York, New York 10011.

ISBN 0-7172-6753-9

Printed in the U.S.A.
First printing, February 2003

Disney's

101 Dalmatians II

Patch's London Adventure

SCHOLASTIC INC.

New York   Toronto   London   Auckland   Sydney
Mexico City   New Delhi   Hong Kong   Buenos Aires

Pongo and Perdita shared a small London home
with a rather large family. It consisted of their "pets"
Roger and Anita Radcliffe; Nanny, the housekeeper;
and ninety-nine Dalmatian puppies!

The puppies liked being part of a big family.
But someone had to be last, and that someone was
usually Patch.

This happened one night when Roger called, "Is
everybody ready for the show?"

All the puppies raced into
the living room to watch "The
Thunderbolt Adventure Hour."
Little Patch was last. He
squeezed in just in time to
hear, "Starring Thunderbolt
the One-of-a-Kind Wonder
Dog . . . and his trusty
sidekick, Little Lightning."

In this episode, little Wholesome Tommy was tied to the smokestack of a runaway train.

"Hold on, Tommy! Thunderbolt's coming!" Patch shouted. He leapt closer to the TV to watch Thunderbolt save the day.

Patch wished he could be a one-of-a-kind hero, just like Thunderbolt.

After the show, it was time for bed. But Patch stayed
in the room long enough to hear an announcer talk about
auditions for the Thunderbolt show. "If you think your
pooch has what it takes . . . just follow a Kanine
Krunchies truck down to tomorrow's auditions!"

Patch couldn't believe his luck. "Dad! Dad! I've just gotta see Thunderbolt tomorrow!" he shouted.

"But tomorrow is moving day," Pongo reminded his son. The whole family was moving to the country.

Nanny put a new dog tag around Patch's neck, saying happily, "Cherry Tree Farm. Why, I imagine it's the most splendid farm in the whole country."

Everyone else was happy about the move, too.

Perdita added, "And best of all, we'll be miles away from that evil ugly monster."

Perdita was talking about Cruella De Vil, the woman who had once kidnapped the puppies. Cruella *still* loved spots. In a nearby art gallery, she was staring at a painting of a single spot.

"Where is the artist? I simply must meet him!" Cruella demanded. She hoped spotted art would make her forget about spotted fur.

"I am Lars," the artist announced, "and I'm an undiscovered genius."

The next morning, Patch was still asleep when the moving van arrived to take everyone to the country. He quickly woke up as he heard Roger call, "All right everyone, into the truck."

Racing to the window, Patch saw his brothers and sisters jumping into the truck. Pongo had already lost count. "Right—anyone not here speak up," he said with a laugh.

Pongo didn't notice that Patch was missing. The pup tried to open the window, but it was stuck. Frantically, Patch cried, "Wait for me!"

But he was too late. "They didn't even miss me," Patch sighed as the moving van rumbled down the road without him.

Suddenly Patch spotted the Kanine Krunchies
truck stop near his house! The puppy finally managed
to open the window and squeeze out. He hopped onto
the truck and took off for the Thunderbolt auditions!

After Patch arrived at the audition, the TV producer announced, "Line up your dogs. We need to hear their best heroic bark!"

But when it was Patch's turn, all that came out was a tiny bark. "Say, who sat on the squeaky toy?" joked Thunderbolt. Everybody laughed. Poor Patch had lost his chance to be on the show.

Later, Thunderbolt was in his trailer when Little
Lightning rushed in with terrible news. In their next
show, Thunderbolt was going to die!

Thunderbolt was stunned. What would he do now?

"Wait a minute . . . what if I went out and did
something heroic in the real world!" Thunderbolt
said. The producer would see that Thunderbolt was a
true hero!

So Thunderbolt left his trailer in search of a real adventure. But he didn't know how to find it. Patch spotted his hero and caught up with him. "I'm your biggest fan . . . I know everything about every episode by heart!" Patch told him.

Eventually, Thunderbolt decided Patch just might be able to help him find an adventure. But Thunderbolt didn't tell Patch that he'd never been a *real* hero before.

They walked through the park. There, Thunderbolt mistook a peaceful horse and carriage for a runaway stagecoach! Patch remembered, "This is just like in episode thirty-seven!"

So Thunderbolt jumped into action to save the people! Sadly, he wasn't good at real-life adventures. He frightened the horse, and the people fell into the pond!

None of their other adventures turned out any better.

Back on the set, the producer found out that
Thunderbolt wasn't there. "WHAT DO YOU MEAN
HE'S MISSING?!" he screamed. "How can you shoot
a show without a star?!"

Then Little Lightning secretly slipped
the producer a photo. The producer declared,
"This is megafantabulous! We'll rewrite this
episode to star Little Lightning!"

" 'The Little Lightning Adventure Hour'
has a nice ring, doesn't it?" the jealous
Lightning laughed to himself.

Meanwhile, Lars had tried to create spotted art for Cruella De Vil. But nothing pleased her.

Then Cruella had an idea. Surely the spotted fur of Dalmatian puppies would inspire Lars!

So the next morning, she hurried to Roger and Anita's old home, only to discover that they had moved. "How unspeakably rude!" she ranted.

Cruella had no idea where to find them . . . until she saw a photo of Patch at the Thunderbolt audition in the newspaper. Cruella was able to read the address on Patch's tag!

It wasn't long before Roger saw the same photo of Patch. Stunned, he exclaimed, "What?! Patch in London!"

"This is all my fault. If only I hadn't lost count," Pongo fretted.

"The important thing now is that we find him before Cruella De Vil does!" Perdita said, as they jumped into the car with Roger and Anita. Soon they were speeding back to London.

Unfortunately, Perdita's
worst fears were about to
come true. Cruella had bailed
Jasper and Horace Baddun out of
jail. She wanted them to help her
snatch the puppies—again! Last time, they
had failed horribly. "It's time to finish the
job," she declared.

"We always get the worst end of it
with her," moaned Horace.

Jasper disguised himself as a woman as part of Cruella's plan. When the Kanine Krunchies truck pulled up, the driver asked him, "Somethin' I can do for a pretty young lady like yourself?"

"Of course you can!" Jasper answered sweetly. "You can just . . . GIVE ME THIS TRUCK!" he yelled as he pulled the startled driver out of his truck.

Then Jasper and Horace
drove to the Cherry Tree Farm.
They easily lured all the
puppies into the truck.

But before the Badduns could get
away, Nanny raced toward them.
"Let those puppies go right now or
I'm going to knock the stupid
out of both of you!" she cried,
waving a heavy frying pan!

Racing around the farm, Horace and Jasper were finally able to grab Nanny, tie her up, and lower her down into a well.

"That ought to hold you right proper," Jasper declared.

Then the Badduns hurried off to deliver the puppies to Cruella.

Cruella was pleased
and brought the puppies
to Lars's loft, which
was in a warehouse.

Lars fell in love with
the puppies. "Aren't
you just a sweetie?"
he crooned to one of
the pups. Lars asked
eagerly, "You mean for
me to do a painting of
them, don't you?"

"No!" Cruella
announced. "I want
you to . . . use their
coats as canvasses!"

Horrified, Lars
refused.

Cruella snapped,
"If I can't have a
masterpiece, at least
I'll finally have a
fabulous Dalmatian
  coat!"

Lars fainted at
the thought.

Not long after, Thunderbolt and Patch heard barking. Dogs around the city were trying to tell them something.

"Sounds like a kidnapping . . . being held in a warehouse . . . a devil woman . . . 101 Dalmatians," Thunderbolt translated.

Patch panicked. "That is my family. Cruella must have them again!"

Thunderbolt agreed to help. He barked a message to the barking chain, then he and Patch set off to save the puppies!

Back in the trailer, Little Lightning heard the barking. He found out that Thunderbolt was going to try to save the puppies.

"What if 'Blunder-Bolt' gets lucky and succeeds!" Lightning muttered. If Thunderbolt became a hero, Lightning would never be a star. He had to stop them!

Thunderbolt and Patch
made their way to the
warehouse where Lars
lived. Lightning was
waiting for him.
"Lightning! What are you
doing here?" Thunderbolt
asked, surprised.

"Thought you might need a bit of help,"
Lightning fibbed.

Thunderbolt jumped onto a fire escape and
climbed to the roof. Patch and Lightning followed.

From the roof, Thunderbolt and Patch leapt through a skylight and down into Lars's loft. The other puppies were amazed. "It's Patch. And he brought Thunderbolt!" exclaimed Lucky.

But then Cruella knocked out Thunderbolt. She picked up Patch. "If it wasn't for you, I'd never have found your brothers and sisters . . . and now I have you all!" she laughed wickedly.

When Thunderbolt woke up, he was locked in a cage with Patch. Then Thunderbolt saw his trusty sidekick outside the cage. "Lightning, little buddy!" the big dog whispered.

"I am not your little buddy," Lightning sneered. "And you're no wonder dog."

Patch didn't understand. Thunderbolt was a *real* hero.

Lightning explained, "He was lying to you all day, kid. He was just trying to get his name in the paper and save his job."

Patch was confused. "You lied to me?" he asked.

Thunderbolt admitted, "I put on an act . . . it's what
I do." Then Thunderbolt turned away ashamed. "I'm
sorry, all right? I'm not a real wonder dog. I just acted
like one once."

Patch didn't know what to do now.

Patch admitted sadly to all the puppies, "I am just *one* of a hundred and one. I'm sorry, this is all my fault."

Then Patch remembered a TV episode when Thunderbolt got out of a cage just like the one they were in!

Patch sprang into action and opened the latch! He quickly freed his brothers and sisters.

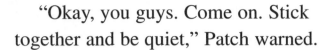

"Okay, you guys. Come on. Stick together and be quiet," Patch warned.

Thunderbolt was too embarrassed to follow. Patch couldn't wait. Just in time, he led his brothers and sisters out of the loft.

When Cruella
discovered that the
puppies had disappeared,
she was furious. "You
let them escape?!"
she yelled at Horace
and Jasper.

Cruella rushed for the
door. "The mutts must
already be downstairs!"

On the street, Patch spotted
an empty double-decker bus
whose driver had gotten off to
buy a newspaper.

Patch sneaked the puppies on
board. "Come on, we're gonna
hitch a ride!" Patch urged.

The puppies accidentally knocked the bus into gear. The bus rolled away down the hill!

"There they are!" Cruella screamed. "GET THEM!" Cruella jumped into the Kanine Krunchies truck with Horace and Jasper.

The runaway bus roared right through the middle of London. Brave little Patch did his best to steer the bus as Cruella and the Badduns came closer and closer.

Meanwhile, Little Lightning was ready
to film his first big scene. The producer said,
"OK, quiet on the set . . . ACTION!"

Just then the
Dalmatians' bus smashed
through the set!
Wholesome Tommy
jumped away. But
Lightning ended up
plastered to the front
of the bus, holding
on for dear life!

Patch finally managed to stop the bus before it crashed in an alley. Lightning promptly fainted. Then Patch directed his brothers and sisters to the open windows of a building. "You go ahead. I'll hold them off . . . somehow," he said as Cruella, Horace, and Jasper closed in.

But little Patch was no match for Cruella and the Badduns. No one could save Patch now except . . .

. . . Thunderbolt! Patch was amazed.

Thunderbolt winked. "C'mon—I always arrive just in the nick of time!"

Cruella grabbed a tire iron from Jasper and swung it at Thunderbolt.

Thunderbolt fell down. Lightning raced over.

"DO NOT MOURN ME WHEN I AM GONE. Goodbye . . . old . . . friend," Thunderbolt whispered dramatically.

Thinking fast, Patch released the brake on the bus.
It rolled down the alley . . . and at the last minute,
Thunderbolt jumped aside! He wasn't dead. He had
been acting! But the runaway bus forced the villains to
jump into a river!

The police soon arrived with Nanny. "THERE they
are. Those are the ones!" Nanny shouted.

Horace and Jasper pointed at Cruella and cried,
"She made us do it!" The police hauled them all away.

Roger, Anita, Pongo, and Perdita were happily reunited with Patch and the other puppies. "We missed you very much, Patch," Pongo declared. Then Pongo thanked Thunderbolt.

Patch was amazed when Thunderbolt said, "No, no. It was your son, Patch." He looked at the pup and said, "You are a real One-of-a-Kind Wonder Dog!"

Pongo added proudly, "And you always were, son."

Thunderbolt went back to being a TV star. But now he had a new Junior Deputy—Patch. They continued to save people—with help from all the other Dalmatian puppies.

And once Patch finally realized he was definitely a One-of-a-Kind Dog, he no longer barked like a squeaky toy.